Welcome aboard, Baby Rio Commagere.
Our boat is much better with you in it.
— B. S.

Text and illustrations copyright © 2021 Barney Saltzberg
Cover and internal design by Simon Stahl

Library of Congress Control Number: 2021930928

Published by Creston Books, LLC
www.crestonbooks.co

ISBN 978-1-939547-96-5
Source of Production: 1010 Printing
Printed and bound in China
5 4 3 2 1

MIX
Paper from
responsible sources
FSC® C016973

'RE ALL IN THE SAME BOAT!

BARNEY SALTZBERG

What do we say when a dog and a cat
go rowing together with a pig and a goat?

What happens when we don't agree on which direction to go?

What happens if one of us wants to splash?

What happens when someone rocks the boat?

What happens if our boat springs a leak?

What happens if we are caught in a rainstorm?

What do we do when the waves get big?

What happens if one of us falls in?

What do we do...